POOR
BADGER

POOR BADGER

K. M. PEYTON

ILLUSTRATED BY MARY LONSDALE

Delacorte Press

Published by
Delacorte Press
Bantam Doubleday Dell Publishing Group, Inc.
666 Fifth Avenue
New York, New York 10103

This work was originally published in Great Britain in 1990
by Doubleday, a division of Transworld Publishers Ltd.

Text copyright © 1990 by K. M. Peyton

Illustrations copyright © 1990 by Mary Lonsdale

Library of Congress Cataloging in Publication Data

Peyton, K. M.
  Poor Badger / K. M. Peyton; illustrated by Mary Lonsdale.
    p.   cm.
  Summary: Having become passionately devoted to a pony who
is being mistreated by his owner, nine-year-old Ros decides to
steal him in the night and hide him in a place of safety.
  ISBN 0-385-30561-3
  [1. Ponies—Fiction. 2. Animals—Treatment—Fiction.]
I. Lonsdale, Mary, ill. II. Title.
PZ7.P4483Po   1992
[Fic]—dc20   91-18404 CIP AC

Design by Diane Stevenson—SNAP·HAUS GRAPHICS

Manufactured in the United States of America

March 1992

10 9 8 7 6 5 4 3 2 1

BVG

TO HANNAH

POOR BADGER

CHAPTER

1

Going home from school, the path led out of
Safeway's parking lot and across a wide stretch
of rough ground toward the railroad. It was
spring and the ground was greening happily,
bright with dandelions and—

"Hey, look!"

Ros stopped in her tracks and Leo, trailing,
walked into the back of her.

"What?"

"Look!" Her voice quivered with glory.
"Look!" It squeaked, out of control.

Leo looked. Usually the field was empty, ex-
cept perhaps for an old man walking his dog,
but today a pony was grazing in it, held by a
chain fastened to a tether. It was, even Leo
could see, a very spectacular pony. It was black
and white, a circus pony, very round and strong-

looking. When it saw them staring, it lifted its head and surveyed them with a bold look from beneath a long, thick forelock. It took several paces toward them, as far as its tether would allow, and let out a soft nickering sound of friendliness. At least, it sounded like friendliness.

"Isn't he gorgeous!"

Ros stood rooted in admiration. She was crazy about ponies, Leo knew, just as he was crazy about frogs. But the pony was, indeed, gorgeous. Although standing still, he seemed to exude vitality. His eyes shone. His coat shone. His round hooves, planted squarely, gleamed as if they had been rubbed with polish. His black bits shone like coal and his white bits like silver.

Ros was enchanted. She was nine, a tough, amiable girl whom the shy Leo was glad to have as a friend (and protector). He was happy to go along where she led and, if she thought the pony amazing, so would he.

"Yes," he said.

"Let's talk to him."

Ros approached, holding out her hand.

"I wish I had an apple or something."

Leo kept well behind.

The pony made his nickering noise again and

reached out to Ros. She went up close and the
pony pushed at her arm quite strongly, and
wobbled his lips at her hand. But the chain
stopped him, fastened to a collar around his
neck. Ros stroked his nose, a bit nervously at
first, then more confidently. Leo kept out of
range. The grass all around the pony was trampled down, as if he had walked about a lot. The

trampling made a perfect circle around the tether pin.

"Isn't he beautiful!" Ros glowed with joy, as if he were hers. "Isn't he marvelous? Where's he come from? Whose is he?"

"He wasn't here this morning," Leo said, not very cleverly.

The pony shoved and rubbed at Ros, but didn't bite. He was strong and pushy, but kind (like Ros, Leo thought. They were a good match).

"He needs moving," Ros said. "He's squashed all his grass."

"His owner will come and do it," Leo said.

"Yes. I'm going to come back after tea and bring him an apple, and perhaps his owner will be here then. We can find out what his name is."

"What would you call him, if he was yours?"

They walked on home, considering this question.

"You could call him Jigsaw. Or Jester."

Leo thought of his nature book, and the picture of a black face with a white stripe, like the pony's.

"I would call him Badger."

Ros wished she'd thought of this.

"Yes, that suits him."

"Shall we call him Badger, then?" Leo asked, pleased.

"Yes. We'll call him Badger." Ros was a bit annoyed because she hadn't thought of it herself. But it was too good to turn down.

"Are you coming back later?"

"No, I've got a music lesson."

"Ugh!" Ros made a disgusted but sympathetic noise. Leo was forced by his parents to do uplifting things, more than she was.

They crossed the railroad by the footbridge. It had high metal fences on either side at the top so you couldn't lean over and drop things on the trains. At the far side they had to cross a busy two-lane highway that ran alongside the railroad. They had been well trained to walk down to the automatic crossing, press the button, and wait until the light turned green for them, and stopped the cars.

They had been doing the journey on their own for two years, since they were seven. Their mothers had taken a lot of trouble to train them to be very careful about the railroad and the two-lane highway, but once across those, they needn't bother anymore, because they only had to cross another field, with cows in, and go into their back gardens by gates their fathers had built in the fence. They lived three houses apart, their houses being in a higgledy-piggledy row of six old cottages, once lived in by railroad workers and farm laborers. Now the cottages had been made rather attractive, and had had garages built in their gardens.

"What time are you going to see Badger?" Leo asked, trying out the new name. He stood with his hand on his garden gate.

"Six o'clock."

"That's the time I have my lesson."

"Bad luck," said Ros, not unkindly.

But she wasn't sorry she would be going on her own. Leo didn't feel the same as she did about Badger, she knew that. To her, Badger was a fantastic bonus in her unexciting life: she had him to look forward to every day, with any luck, and she could get to know him, and he her, and feed him apples and be his friend. She couldn't have riding lessons, because her parents said they couldn't afford it. Ros didn't whine or argue because, with her parents, it never made any difference. Instead, she had imaginary ponies, written down in a book, with names, and she collected pictures of racehorses for her own imaginary string. She went to horse shows, and pretended all the winners were hers, really—she just let other people ride them. She pretended it all. It was hard work. But now, suddenly, there was real Badger.

Perhaps whoever owned him wanted a rider for him . . . perhaps a kind old man had bought him who was looking for a little girl to exercise him . . . Ros's imagination started work again. She saw herself, crash helmet over her eyes, galloping over the fields on Badger. She had never actually sat on a pony, but in her imagination she could ride like the blond and smiling British heroines of the Olympic Games.

"Hey, Mom, what do you think?"

She crashed into the kitchen and poured it all out.

"How do you know it's called Badger?" her mother asked.

"I—we—called it Badger!"

"Oh. Very nice."

Her mother was a strict and homely woman called Dora, once a farmer's daughter. She worked now as a part-time secretary at the local secondary school, and was usually home well before Ros. She regretted not being able to afford a pony for Ros, but she liked animals, and they had two cats, a dog called Erm, some rabbits, and Leo's wretched frogs in the garden pond. Leo's mother, Mrs. Cross (she was rather suitably named), had refused to let Leo dig a pond in his garden, so he had dug one in theirs instead. Ros's father Harry had helped him line it with a plastic sheet and fill the bottom with earth and gravel and plant it with frog cover: water lilies and reeds from the garden center. From frogspawn there had been tadpoles, and now frogs . . . it had all been a great success. Leo spent hours in their garden. The cats, having caught a few small frogs at first, now ignored them. They didn't like the taste. Harry had to be very careful when he mowed the lawn. Leo went ahead of him, anxiously looking.

"I'm going to take him an apple after tea."

"Take a carrot. Apples cost too much."

Her mother found her two large ones, and cut them up and put them in a bag. She showed her how to offer food to ponies, with the palm held uppermost, the tidbit lying in the middle.

"He doesn't bite. He's very friendly." Ros knew about palm uppermost anyway. Grown-ups were always telling you things you already knew.

"Your father's going to be late. You needn't wait for him. I'll get your tea now."

Dora Palfrey understood about things, which was more than Leo's mother usually did. (Ros liked her surname being Palfrey. It was an old-fashioned word for a riding horse, the sort medieval ladies had ridden on, draperies trailing. She liked her name actually meaning "horse." It was a great privilege.)

Mrs. Palfrey fixed Ros her favorite fish sticks and French fries, and Ros changed into jeans and parka and set off back to see Badger, the carrots stuffed in her parka pockets. It was a fine evening with a strong smell of spring and the blackbirds singing in the hedges. Ros felt very cheerful, having discovered a pony that was almost her own, so close and friendly. But when she came over the railroad bridge she saw that the pony was no longer alone, and she stopped, deeply disappointed.

There was a family with him: a dad, a mom and four children. They were all rather noisy and excited. The mom was trying to calm them down and the dad was putting a saddle on Badger. Badger was circling restlessly and a girl of about eleven was hanging on to his head, shouting at the others to keep out of the way. As a family, they seemed to use a lot of swear words, although they were laughing a lot too.

Ros went nearer. It was public ground, after all. She stood on the path, her hand closed around the carrots in her pocket.

The girl was the eldest. She was very active and tough, and had a mass of thick, wiry hair that looked like a pot scrubber on her head. She squashed a riding hat over it and hooked up the harness. Her father bunked her up into the saddle.

"Hold on now, Fi!"

Badger was barging about in great excitement, pawing the ground and snatching at his bit. He looked nothing like a child's "first pony." But Fi's dad was laughing, and let go without seeming to have any doubts, although Mom looked a bit worried. Badger plunged away and came straight toward where Ros was standing, at a very fast trot. He lifted his knees high and held his head up and snorted as he went, looking very flashy and strong.

Fi was hauling on the reins to steady him, but did not seem frightened. She saw Ros standing there and shouted, "Watch out!" in a very imperious, bossy voice, but Ros did not move. She had as much right there as Fi, and Badger liked her, she knew. She wasn't frightened. Fi shouted something rude to her and steered Badger past. His eyes were shining with half excitement, half fear, Ros thought. He looked barely under control. But Fi was strong too, and not afraid.

"Ride 'im, Fi!" her father shouted. "You show the little devil!"

The girl and the pony seemed well matched. They were both fit and strong and bossy, and Fi circled and cantered and even galloped, and her family stood watching and applauding and shouting rude remarks. It was all very jolly. When Fi had got Badger tired, all the other children had a turn, even the little one, with Dad running beside and crying out, "Of course you can trot—there's nothing to it! Up, down! Up, down! Hold on, you little so-and-so!"

Ros stood there until it was nearly dark.

When they had finished, they put Badger back on his tether again and brought him a bucket of water from the car. Then, trailing the saddle and bridle, they all piled into a large car on the edge of the parking lot and drove away.

CHAPTER

2

When they had gone, Ros went across to Badger. This time he looked at her rather nervously, not in his friendly, eager way of the first time. Ros rather got the message—"Oh, not again!"

"It's me, Badger. I've brought you some carrots."

Although his owners had moved his tether peg, the grass was still rather trampled. The whole field looked rather trampled. And Badger had already drunk nearly all of the bucket of water they had left him. The pony's coat was curly with sweat, and hot and damp under Ros's hand. But the air had gone cool and sharp with the onset of dusk.

"I can't stay, Mom'll be furious," Ros told him. She wanted to. She didn't think Badger was happy. He was all stirred up with the fast rid-

ing, and moved about restlessly, pulled up sharp
all the time by the tether. Ros talked to him
softly, and she thought her presence soothed
him. When she left him, he walked after her to
the end of the chain, and stood and watched until she was out of sight. He whinnied after her
once. She heard the whinny in her head all the
way home.

"I was just about to send out a search party!" her mother said, annoyed (but not too annoyed). "You can't have been talking to a pony all that time?"

Ros explained.

It was hard to say exactly why, but she felt cast down by her evening. She didn't like Fi very much, and Badger belonged to Fi. She tried to tell her mother this.

"Well, they wouldn't buy a pony if they didn't want him, which means they must like ponies, doesn't it?"

"I suppose so."

But her father Harry said, "Funny place to keep one, all the same. They're not gypsies, from the sound of them."

"Well, that ground was part of a common, once. Before Safeway's. It was all common land, before the railroad and the arterial highway. I think they've got right on their side."

"Could get stolen."

"You'd have to take him through the town to get away! Out through the parking lot. I can't see anyone risking that."

"I suppose not."

When Ros was in bed, she lay thinking about Badger. In the morning she was off early for school, with more carrots in her bag. Leo wasn't ready, and she wouldn't wait.

Badger was standing with his head down, dozing, not looking as handsome as the day before. His coat was curled and stiff with dried sweat. His water bucket was empty and kicked aside. But he was very pleased with the carrots and snuffled at Ros in his friendly way. Ros was longing to spend the day with him, take him for a walk to find some nice grass, and groom his lovely coat back to its sleek shine. But she knew Fi or Fi's dad would come soon and see to him, move his tether peg, and bring him some water.

But when she came home from school in the afternoon, no one had been there. His kicked bucket lay where it had been in the morning, he was ungroomed and unmoved. He whinnied to her when he saw her, quite anxiously, she thought.

Ros went up and stroked and patted him, but she had given him all the carrots in the morning.

"I'll bring two batches tomorrow," she said to him. "And I'll come back tonight."

Fi and her dad must come soon, she thought, to look after him. He had no grass, only a beaten-down mud patch. She was worried about

him, and started to dream that Fi and her dad
never came back, and looking after Badger fell
to her and after a while he became hers . . .

She told her mother about it all and her
mother said, "He must be terribly thirsty by
now. They're bound to be back to see to him."

"Can I go?"

"Yes. Look, I bought more carrots on the way
home. But you mustn't be so late tonight. You've
got your homework to do."

Ros gobbled her tea and ran.

When she got back to Badger, the family was
just arriving, this time just Dad and Fi and two
of the small children, no Mom. Dad pulled a
five-gallon water container out of his car trunk
and filled Badger's bucket, and Badger drank
the whole bucketful in one gulp.

"You thirsty little fellow!" Dad exclaimed.
"You've drunk the whole thing!"

He sounded most surprised. But without more
ado he put the saddle and bridle on and bunked
Fi up on Badger's back. Once more Fi trotted
and cantered around and around the field until
Badger was covered with sweat, then Dad
propped a pole up on a couple of oil cans and Fi
jumped backward and forward over it, with
much applause from her brothers and encour-

agement from Dad. Badger was a very good jumper, Ros noted, but he got very excited and started to pull hard at Fi's strong hands. Fi had obviously done plenty of riding and was in no danger of falling off, but she was a very hard and unsympathetic rider and, when Badger started to pull, she sat back and heaved on the reins. Badger pulled back and started to gallop. Fi steered him in a circle, hauling viciously on the inside rein, and eventually Badger came to a halt.

"The little devil!" Dad shouted. "I thought he was supposed to be well mannered!"

"He's terribly strong!" Fi said, looking slightly anxious.

"Yeah, too strong. If we give him less food, he'll quiet down, I reckon. We'll teach him, eh?"

So Dad did not move Badger's tether peg, leaving the pony without any grass at all, nor did he refill the empty bucket, whether because he thought one bucket a day was enough, or whether to teach the pony a lesson Ros could not tell.

When they had gone, Ros stood miserably feeding Badger his carrots. She was now far more than anxious, in fact slightly desperate.

"I shall move you, dear Badger. You can't go all night without any grass!"

It was a terrible struggle getting the tether pin out. While she was trying, the old man who walked his dog came by. He lived in one of the houses that backed onto the waste ground at the far end, and Ros had always said hello to him. His name was Albert. He was a gloomy sort of man but his dog was nice and got lots of walks, Albert not having much to do all day and used to an outdoor life.

"Watcha up to, then?"

Ros told him, and he helped her. They took the peg to some new grass, not too far, in case Dad noticed. Ros didn't think he would.

"Funny way to keep a pony," Albert said.

"They've left him without water!"

"Aye, well, bring the bucket along and I'll fill it for 'im," Albert said.

Ros walked with Albert to his back-garden gate, carrying the bucket. She felt terribly relieved at the offer. Albert had worked on a farm most of his life, and knew about horses. Ros waited outside his back door while he filled the bucket.

"Can you manage it?" He sounded doubtful.

"Yes. Yes, of course."

It was very heavy, but she managed to struggle back to Badger without spilling much. Her feet were a bit soggy, that's all. Badger plunged his nose in and drank about three quarters of the water.

Ros was pleased with her work, although still very anxious about Badger's treatment from his owners. Not giving him any food was bound to quiet him down, but surely there were better ways of soothing a high-spirited pony. But she had no time to linger. She had to run all the way home so that her mother wouldn't be upset.

She told her parents all about it.

"Sounds like they're a little ignorant," said her mother. "There's a lot of cruelty to animals comes about by ignorance."

Their dog Erm, now very ancient, had come from the animal shelter. Her real name was Ermintrude and when they first had her, she was very stupid and thin, because she had been shut in a shed and left all day and all night, but after living in a family and being treated properly for a while she became very intelligent and loving. But she was too old now to go as far as Badger's field, and Ros only took her for short walks down the lane.

"What can I do about Badger?" Ros asked her parents.

"He's not yours. Nothing," they said.

"Not yet, anyway," said her father.

Her mother ruffled Ros's hair affectionately. "They must *want* him, after all. He'll be all right."

And with that Ros had to be content.

CHAPTER

3

The evenings continued in the same fashion, Ros going to see Badger and Fi coming to ride him.

Fi said to Ros, "Stary cat! What you always staring for?"

"Who's going to stop me, Bighead?"

Ros was no faintheart. She felt bitter toward Fi and her family for the brutish way they treated Badger. Badger was becoming more nervous and less friendly, and put his ears back now when once he had come forward with his little nicker of greeting.

"But you love me, don't you, Badger?" Ros asked him anxiously, making up his diet with carrots and a bagful of porridge oats she had filched from the pantry. Once he saw who it was, Badger rubbed his head against her arm in his old friendly way.

He wasn't as round and shining as he had been. His summer coat was scurfy and he was thin in the flanks. If it wasn't for herself and Albert, filling his bucket every day, he would have died of thirst before now, Ros thought. Albert had had a talk with Fi's dad, but he had told Albert to keep his long nose out of business that didn't concern him.

"They are horrid people. I hate them!" Ros told her mother.

Her mother was sorry that what had started as a great thrill and interest for Ros had turned sour for her. She knew that it was making Ros unhappy, seeing Badger badly treated, but there wasn't anything she could do about it. It wasn't bad enough for the SPCA.

"After all, although he's on a tether, strictly speaking they do go and see him every day, and move him. He's not exactly neglected."

"But there's hardly any grass, even when they do move him. They've ridden it all down."

One evening, overhearing Fi's conversation with her dad, Ros found out that they were taking Badger to a horse show the next weekend, to enter him in a jumping category. Ros pricked up her ears, and decided to go too.

Leo said he would come with her.

"You could enter Andrew," Ros said, grinning.

Andrew was the boss frog. Ros didn't see how Leo could tell them apart, but Leo swore he could. Andrew had a spot on his back; he was the only one Ros could tell was different, but Leo had names for lots of them. Ros suspected he just said the names to impress her.

Harry gave them a lift to the horse show, which was about ten miles away. It was in a huge field, where lines of horse trailers were pulled up, and rings roped off for jumping and showing and the gymkhana. Ros knew about horse shows, and where to look, but Leo was very ignorant. He even thought small ponies were just young horses, and would grow into big horses later on.

"Stupid! Ponies are ponies and horses are horses, however old they are!"

"Well, nobody ever told me! If no one had ever told you, you wouldn't know a tadpole would grow into a frog. Would you?"

Ros scowled.

"Would you?" Leo persisted.

"Not if no one had said, no. You wouldn't think so."

"Well, then. No one ever said to me about ponies."

He trailed after her in his baggy shorts and baby Disney-decorated T-shirt, and Ros tried to be nice to him. She had lots of good friends at school but none of them were crazy about horses, like her, and all had refused to come to the horse show. At least Leo, however pathetic he was, seemed to understand about Badger. He brought him carrots too, and once a whole box of muesli he stole out of the pantry.

Ros bought a program. She saw Fi, dressed very smartly in a black jacket and boots, and wearing the number 137. Ros looked her up in the program.

"Hey!" she said, finding it. "Do you know what Badger's name is?"

"What? What is it?"

"Mountfitchet Meteor Light!"

Leo looked puzzled. "Is that a name?"

"That's what it says."

"It sounds like a firework."

"Fi's is Fiona Smith."

It was a hot day and people were sitting around the jumping ring on bales of straw. The jumps looked enormous, but little ponies seemed to be whizzing over them without any trouble. Ros could see Badger in the collecting ring, prancing about in a very spirited manner. Fi was holding him hard with her viselike hands, and Dad Smith was standing there in his shirtsleeves, grinning and geeing them up. There was a practice jump that Fi did several times, and Badger was getting more and more excited.

When he came into the ring, Fi had to wait a while for some jumps to be put up again after the previous pony. While she was waiting, Ros heard a woman behind her say to her friend, "Good Lord, that's dear old Meteor Light! I'd never have recognized him! Who on earth's got him now?"

"Oh, some very ignorant people bought him. Doesn't he look poor? It was criminal not to make sure he went to a good home, after being such a brilliant winner for that family—all the ribbons they collected with him!"

"They were asking a big price though."

"Yes, and these people paid it!"

"But what have they done to him? He looks so poor."

"Probably the girl can't manage him when he's fit."

At this point in the conversation, Fi got the whistle to start her round, and Badger leapt into action and bore down on the first jump. He was a brilliant jumper, but Ros could see that Fi had very little control over him. He went much too fast, and after jumping the first three he went too fast around the corner at the end and Fi could not settle him down in time for the fourth. He went straight past it and raced toward the next. Fi had to haul him back and take him around in a circle.

The lady behind Ros said, in a stern voice, "What a horrid spectacle! That child's got no idea!"

Fi came up to the jump at such an angle that Badger could not see what to do and stopped dead. Fi shot over the jump on her own and landed in a heap.

Leo laughed. "Serves her right!"

"Shut up, Leo!" Ros felt as if she was sitting on pins. Poor Badger! He cantered around the ring and someone caught him and took him back to Fi. Fi got up looking murderous. She was legged back on. She gave Badger two tremendous whacks with her whip and Badger bucked. Fi managed to stay on. She turned him in another circle and presented him at the jump again, and this time Badger jumped so big that Fi bounced right out of the saddle and landed on his neck, her hands clutching feverishly at his ears. Badger put his head down, bucked again, and Fi landed on the ground once more.

"Oh, really! What a farce!" said the woman behind Ros. "The poor animal's doing his best, but that idiot girl can't ride!"

This time Badger dashed out of the ring and Dad Smith caught him in the collecting ring. Fi got up and ran out of the ring. Dad Smith obviously wanted her to go back in and "get her money's worth" but Fi burst into tears and refused. Her father, looking very red and angry, grabbed her by the arm and marched her away from the interested spectators, trailing Badger behind.

Ros got up to go.

"What are you doing?" Leo asked, following.

"I'm going to see what they do."

Leo came with her. Ros felt as if she was burning inside. She pushed through the crowd. Mr. Smith led Badger back to where a large horse trailer was parked in line with the others. It was quiet here, and there was no one about, only a few ponies tied up picking at their hay-racks. Mr. Smith was in a terrible temper. He took Badger's saddle off and threw it on the ground, then he lifted his hand and cuffed Badger about the ears. Badger pulled back, but Mr. Smith jerked viciously at his mouth and said, "You want to be taught a lesson, you brute!" He pulled Fi's whip out of her hand and struck Badger cruelly across the face.

Ros, having followed closely behind, could not contain her rage.

"Stop it!" she roared. "You beastly man!"

She launched herself at Mr. Smith and flailed at his massive back with her fists.

He turned around in amazement and fury.

"I'll report you!" Ros screamed at him. "I'll tell the judge! You are cruel and beastly!"

"The heck I am! Shut yer mouth, girl!"

Mr. Smith looked around hastily and then lifted his hand menacingly to Ros. "You clear off, you little interfering madam, before I smack you one on the chops!"

"It's that stary cat, Dad." Fi sniffed.

"Oh, our little Miss Interfering Snotty Nose, is it? Where's yer mom and dad, girl? They ought to take care of you, instead of letting you loose

in public! Where do you live, girl? Tell me that! What's your name?"

He towered over Ros, suddenly very menacing. Ros was terrified. She burst into tears.

"What's your name?"

Ros sobbed it out.

"Palfrey! That's rich!" Mr. Smith laughed in a very unpleasant way. "Well, just take me to your mom and dad, Miss Palfrey, and I'll have something to say to them."

Ros shook with tears and fear. But at this moment a girl rode up to the next-door horse trailer and dismounted. She didn't take any notice of the fraught little group around Badger, but Mr. Smith had to lower his voice.

"You haven't heard the last of this, my girl! Now, run along, or I'll call a policeman."

"It's you that needs a policeman!" Leo said, very bravely, and going very red in the face. But all the same, he was already retreating as he spoke. "Come along, Ros."

They crept away along the line of horse trailers. Ros was sobbing with rage and hurt.

Leo said sadly, "Don't cry, Ros. Badger'll be all right. He won't dare hit him again, with people there."

"Poor darling Badger, belonging to that horrible man! What can we do to help him?"

"Well, we give him carrots." Leo decided to filch another box of muesli that very night. His mother kept a good stock. "We could steal him away."

"Where to?"

"We could look for somewhere."

"Do you think we could?"

"You can do anything if you try hard enough," Leo said, quoting a favorite saying of his father's. He only repeated it; he didn't think it was true.

It didn't sound hopeful, even to Ros, thinking of the railroad line and the arterial highway, not to mention Safeway's parking lot, all hemming Badger in. And besides, stealing was wicked. But not as wicked as Dad Smith.

The show was ruined for Ros, and she went home on the bus with Leo early. Her mother was surprised, and Ros told her what had happened, but she didn't tell her about how she had shouted at Mr. Smith. She pretended she had only watched.

When it was quite late she slipped out to see Badger. He was standing dejectedly on his tether, and shifted uneasily when he saw her, as if he didn't trust anybody anymore, even her. She hugged him and gave him her tidbits. His water bucket was half full. Probably Albert had filled it. The saddle marks were still on his back. No one had bothered to rub him down and make him comfortable. He had hardly anything to eat.

"I do wish you were mine, Badger!"

Now that he had given Fi such a bad time in the show-ring, perhaps he would be sold. But he didn't look half the pony he had looked a few months ago. Ros remembered the shining, bouncy animal she had first set eyes on, roaming around his chain and whinnying. Now he always stood in a head-down, dejected way. Who would want him now? He looked like a cheap pony now, and would quite likely go to another poor home. Or could anybody be as bad as Mr. Smith?

No, she had reason to decide very soon afterward. When she went indoors the telephone rang, and she answered it, hoping it was one of her school friends. But it was Mr. Smith. She recognized his coarse, angry voice right away.

"I want to speak to your father!" he said.

Ros put the receiver back and cut him off. But it rang again shortly and her father came out and picked the receiver up.

Ros went upstairs to her bedroom and sat on her bed, shivering. The thought of Mr. Smith and his cruel expression was unbearable.

As she knew would happen, her father came up to her bedroom after the phone call and said to her, "What's all this then, about your attacking Mr. Smith? Is it true?"

Ros explained, between her hiccuping tears.

Her father listened patiently, his face grave.

"It was wrong of you, but I do understand. I think you ought to keep out of his way in future."

"But I must go and see Badger! He needs me!"

"Look, Ros, you've got to accept that you can't manage the world to suit yourself. You can't interfere. Badger is not yours. He's not well treated, but he's not actually knocked around. If he's starving, as you say, he doesn't look it. Poor, admitted, but not at death's door. I am very much afraid, in spite of what you think, that the people whose job it is to investigate these things, the police or the SPCA, would consider you were wasting their time if you told them about Badger. If you like, I will contact the SPCA and tell them the situation. They might have a word with Mr. Smith. But on the other hand, if they do, he might get fed up and send Badger to market, and who knows what might happen to him there."

"The meat man?"

Ros threw herself down on her bed and wept.
Her father tried to cheer her up, but to himself he had to admit that Ros had gotten herself
into a pretty miserable situation.

CHAPTER

4

After the horse show Fi didn't come to ride Badger anymore. Sometimes the little brothers and sister came, and now Badger was so run-down he didn't buck them off. They trotted around and tried to make him go faster, but he hadn't the spirit anymore, because he hadn't enough food. They drummed on his sides with their heels and he would lurch into a weary canter, and they would shout and hit him with a stick.

Ros had been sternly warned by her father to keep out of Mr. Smith's way. She was frightened of him, anyway.

But she lay on the top of the railroad bank behind the fence and watched through the long grass. Badger was getting thinner and thinner with the treatment he received. Soon, Ros thought, the SPCA would think he was worth

bothering with. Her father had told them, and they had seen Mr. Smith, they said, and the result was that Mr. Smith filled the water bucket more often, and sometimes brought some hay, but only sometimes. It was bad hay, not worth eating. Badger picked at it, and Mr. Smith said it showed he didn't need it.

Mr. Smith guessed who had told the SPCA.

Leo said to Ros, "He'll skin you alive if he sees you."

"Don't be silly!"

But she was frightened all the same.

When the weather started to get colder, she feared for Badger. Mr. and Mrs. Palfrey feared for Ros.

"If only she didn't have to pass the wretched pony every day, she would forget about it! It makes her so miserable!"

"It's a very sad situation. But we can't do anything about it! We can't afford to buy him, and Smith would be very unlikely to sell to us anyway—not the way he thinks about us!"

"No. There's no way we can buy him."

"I can't think of anything we can do."

One night in November, it started to snow. "Very early for snow!" said Ros's father, pulling the curtains across. They all sat around a coal fire, watching television.

When Ros went to bed, she lay watching the snowflakes drifting across her bedroom window, thinking of Badger. She was warm and comfortable and had her mother and father next door, but Badger was cold and hungry and alone, and had nothing to look forward to. There was the whole winter to go yet.

Ros sat up.

"I will do something," she decided. She couldn't go on feeling so miserable about Badger, and not doing anything. Not for the whole winter! It was too long. She wasn't a worm, after all. At school she was known as bossy and resourceful, and yet when it came to Badger she was just useless. And Badger deserved more than that.

"I'll steal him away, and put him somewhere nice," she decided.

"You can't!" Leo said the next day.

"I can. I've only told you because I might want some help, not so that you can say stupid things like that. No one will know who's done it, not if we do it in the middle of the night, and take care no one sees us."

Leo considered.

"In the middle of the night?"

"It would have to be, I think."

"The parking lot is lit up all night. You can see it from here. And the police drive through it, my dad says, to stop the public toilets from getting vandalized."

The parking lot was the only way out of the rough field, apart from the footbridge over the railroad. One side was all houses, and the other had a high wire fence and the back of an industrial park.

"I'll work it out," Ros said defiantly.

The idea, having taken hold, possessed her.

"The only way out is over the footbridge, and across the main road," Leo said. "You can't do that!"

"Who says I can't?"

"Mr. Smith will know it's you."

"He'll have to prove it. We'll leave no clues. No clues at all."

Leo didn't like the "we." He wriggled anxiously.

Ros, softening, said, "Honestly, Leo. It will work if we plan it very carefully. I will think it out."

"Like a general?"

"Yes, like a general." General Palfrey. It sounded good. Badger could depend on General Palfrey.

Armies had training exercises. She would have a training exercise.

"I'll have a practice! I'll try it out, going to Badger when everyone is asleep! I'll try it!"

"When? Tonight?"

"Tonight!" Ros was startled. The snow lay slushy and uninviting over the damp fields and sleet was forecast. But the title she had just given herself put the prospect in a different light.

"Yes. Why not? Tonight. I will go tonight!"

"Me too?" Leo's voice was deeply apprehensive.

"Not this time, no."

"What shall I do, then?"

Ros considered.

"We've got to find somewhere to take him to. That's going to be tricky. You could think about that." Leo was good at thinking. He got high marks at school. He wasn't a lot of good at doing, though.

"Over this way would be easiest, not far from home," she said.

"You'll never get him over the bridge!"

Generals overcame all obstacles. Ros was not going to make the bridge an obstacle. She stuck out her jaw.

"Why not?"

The idea, having take root, would not leave her. But as the day wore on, she decided to shelve the practice run . . . not tonight, anyway. The thought of it, even just the practice, frightened her quite a lot. She must have time to get up her courage. Finding the place to take him to could be tackled first. It was the most important thing, after all.

"We'll go looking on Saturday," she decided. "Both of us. And when we've found a place, I'll have the practice."

She studied the footbridge carefully the next morning on the way to school. Leo was right. It was the only way to take Badger; the parking lot was out of the question, leading as it did into the main shopping center. The footbridge was not used much, even in daytime, and Ros thought it was unlikely they would meet anyone after midnight. Crossing the main road would be tricky, as cars went along it more or less all night. Perhaps at three in the morning there would be a gap, after late-night parties, before work . . .

The footbridge was stoutly built, and the steps up and down were shallow and fairly wide so that bicycles and strollers could be manhandled without too much difficulty.

"You will go over it, won't you, Badger?"

Badger gobbled her carrots greedily and pushed at her pockets for more. Ros thought that for food he would follow her anywhere, now that he was so hungry. If they took a bucket of carrots and oats, and Leo walked in front . . . she would need Leo.

She told him that. He looked wan.

On Saturday they took their bikes and went exploring, to find a place. It needed to be as close as possible, so that they could get home and back in bed without being discovered. The land on their side of the main road was all farms, but mostly crops, and what cow fields there were were all empty now and the gates padlocked. Although Ros was friendly with all the neighboring farmers, none of them were likely to want to have anything to do with stolen property, even if they were sympathetic. There was a riding school a mile away, but all the ponies were now stabled and the fields empty.

"We could bring him here and leave him in the field." Leo noticed that there was no padlock on the gate. "They'd find him in the morning."

"And tell the police," Ros said darkly.

"Well, anyone would. Anyone honest."

"We want someone dishonest then."

"Sid the Pigman is dishonest," Leo said.

Sid the Pigman lived quite close, in a trailer.

He had been turned out of a farm cottage when the farm had changed hands, but had been given the use of a field and a site for a trailer by the farmer. His place was along the arterial highway, separated from it by a wide stretch of scrubby woodland. His trailer had its back to the wood, and looked down the field, which sloped steeply to a stream. He kept a cow and a donkey in the field, and a large barn housed them at night. Half of it was filled with good hay provided by the farmer. The trailer was full of greyhounds, which Sid led out on leashes down the side of the arterial highway, and raced on Saturday nights.

"Who says he's dishonest?" Ros inquired, feeling a lift of interest.

"My dad."

Leo's dad, Ros knew, would assume that anyone who lived in a trailer and raced greyhounds was dishonest. Leo's dad was a terrible snob. He called his cottage Rose Manor End. Rose Manor was the old farmhouse that had been pulled down years ago, and End meant the cottage was the end one of the terrace. But it sounded very elegant. Ros's house was called Enuff. It was called Enuff when they bought it, and her parents thought it was funny and had never bothered to change it. "Enuff money, you can say that again," Harry said. "That's what it means."

Ros asked her dad about Sid the Pigman.

"Leo's dad says he's dishonest."

"Dishonest? Not that I know of. If something came his way, mind you, he wouldn't go looking for the owner."

Ros felt a prickling of anxiety at her father's words. It was almost as if he knew what was in her mind. But he was reading the newspaper at the time and answered in an offhand way, not very interested. He didn't ask her why she wanted to know. His answer fitted Ros's requirements exactly. If he found a piebald pony in his field one morning, he wouldn't go looking for the owner.

The more she thought about Sid the Pigman, the more Ros felt he was the answer to her problem. The riding-school people would be bound to call the police, if she left Badger in their field, but Sid's field was hidden away behind overgrown hedges, and if Sid didn't say anything . . .

"We'll go and spy it out," she said to Leo. "See if it will do."

It was very difficult, the days being dark as soon as they were home from school. She could only do her spying on weekends. If Sid's place was suitable, she decided she would move Badger as soon as possible.

It was now nearly Christmas. School let out for the holidays and the same afternoon they bicycled down the lane to Sid the Pigman and saw that his gate had no padlock on it and that it would be an easy matter to let Badger in. The greyhounds did not bark, and the cow and donkey looked at them serenely. At the top of the field was the barn where the animals could stand out of the rain, and at the bottom a stream of clear running water where they could drink. The grass was good, and the field sheltered by the wood and high hedges. It was a perfect, happy field.

"This is where we'll bring him," Ros said.

"What about your practice?"

Ros rather wished she'd never mentioned the practice. Suppose she was caught practicing? The real thing would then be very difficult. But the General Palfrey tag had taken hold: real campaigns were worked out in great detail. She said nothing to Leo, but put on her general's face, bossy and superior.

"Wait and see."

She knew she had to go.

She must make a decision, and hold to it. There was really no alternative: tonight.

Her parents went to bed at around eleven o'clock, but the traffic on the arterial highway went on until after midnight. The best time to go would be about one o'clock. Ros had an alarm clock but wasn't very good at setting it. She put it under her pillow timed for one o'clock, but if it went off she never heard it, for she didn't wake until five o'clock, by which time it was too late. But while they were having lunch the next day, a frantic burring noise came from upstairs, and Dora Palfrey said, "Whatever's that?" It was just one o'clock.

"It sounds like an alarm clock," Ros said feebly.

Not much of a general . . . lucky Leo didn't know about it.

The next night she determined to stay awake.

She heard her parents come to bed, and lay listening to the wind and rain on the window. She had to stay awake for two more hours. She didn't feel very generallike at all, but during the time she had to think about it, she supposed that generals were quite often as worried as she was about what they were planning. It was a part of being a general, being worried. She dozed off, and awoke with a start. Her clock said ten to one.

She pressed the button to stop the alarm from going off (she hoped), and lay listening. The distant swishes of the cars on the arterial highway were down to almost nothing, and nothing stirred in the house.

She slithered out of bed and got dressed. She had a flashlight, and had arranged her clothes very tidily, in order of putting on, and her parka and rubber boots were handy on the back porch.

She had already prospected squeaking floorboards and had left her bedroom door ajar, and so managed to get downstairs without a sound. She had to go out the back way, through the kitchen, which meant Erm lumbered out of her basket looking expectantly for a walk, even in the middle of the night. Thank goodness she was old and didn't caper about and bark. The only noise she made was a wheeze, and the thump of her tail against the stove.

Ros pushed her to one side and unbolted the kitchen door. The bolt was well oiled and did not make a sound. It was all surprisingly easy. None of the doors stuck or squeaked, and Ros

was out in the garden without any hitches. The night was very dark and cold, with sleet on the wind, but the way was well trodden and the lights from the road cast an orange glow over the field.

Ros set off across the familiar path. She was excited rather than frightened. Her senses seemed much sharper than usual, and she could feel herself shivering, although she wasn't cold. There was a moon that came fleetingly through the flying clouds and disappeared again, but its lightness remained, silvery above the golden glow of the town.

There was no need to use the road crossing, for there were no cars. Ros hopped over the median strip, and was across and climbing the railroad bridge only five minutes after leaving home. It was much quicker, not having to make a detour for the crossing. Over the bridge and, from the top of the steps, she could make out Badger in the moonlight, standing hunch-backed against the wind, his thick tail tucked tightly between his legs. Ros ran down the steps and across the muddy slime of the bedraggled field.

When she got to Badger, she burst into tears.

"Oh, Badger! Poor Badger!" She wept, seeing

him so forlorn in the rain and the wind. Unable to move freely, he had no way of finding shelter or keeping warm. Her pockets were stocked with carrots and old crusts, which he gobbled eagerly. She flung her arms around his neck and wept copiously into his muddy, tangled mane. She could not bear to think of him abandoned day and night with his moldy hay blown away by the wind and his water bucket kicked over. His thick coat barely hid his staring ribs, and his once proud head drooped sadly, all the fire and enthusiasm gone from his eyes. And yet his name was Mountfitchet Meteor Light and he had once been a famous show jumper.

"Why did they sell you to that awful man, Badger?" But Dad Smith had paid the large price, according to the gossiping ladies at the show. The pony's owners had taken their money, and not cared that Dad Smith didn't know anything about how to look after a pony.

They are just as wicked as Mr. Smith, Ros thought, with justice.

She longed to take Badger there and then, and half decided to—then she realized she had nothing to lead him with. The chain was fastened to the leather neck collar with a shackle she hadn't the strength in her fingers to undo, and she could hardly carry all the chain with her. She would have to get a head collar and lead rope before she attempted the real thing.

"Oh, Badger, I will come soon, I promise! I promise!"

She would find herself a head collar that very day.

When she left, the pony followed to the end of his chain and then let out a quite piercing whinny after her. Ros, gulping back the tears, ran for her life. Suppose somebody heard him? But, back on the comparative safety of the railroad bridge, she looked behind and nothing stirred. Nobody cared about Badger's cry of loneliness and despair. Not a person save herself lost any sleep over a starving pony in the winter night.

So much for being bold General Palfrey making a survey of tactics. Ros ran all the way home, not caring who might see her or hear her. Only when she got to her back porch and kicked off her muddy boots, did she remember that she owed it to Badger to complete her practice run successfully. It was terribly important that she got back to bed undiscovered, so that she could safely venture out again on the real mission.

She crept in, bolting the doors behind her.

Erm did not bother to get up this time, only waving her tail vaguely once or twice, and Ros tiptoed upstairs, head down, scratchy with guilt. Nothing stirred. She slipped into her bedroom and threw off her clothes. She still had her pajamas on underneath. Her bed was cold and she couldn't stop shivering, although she felt as if she was burning. She could not get to sleep again, thinking all the time of Badger calling after her.

"I will come tomorrow, Badger, I promise," she whispered into her pillow.

She fell asleep at last, only two hours before she had to get up again. She did not feel very generallike, pulling on her clothes, but her mind was made up.

The campaign was timed for the following night.

CHAPTER

5

Ros crouched beneath the hedge at the bottom of her garden, waiting for Leo. He had had strict instructions to join her at one-thirty. It was now one thirty-five and there was no sign of life from Rose Manor End.

It was very quiet. There was no wind tonight, but the moon was hidden behind heavy cloud and it was very cold. Ros was worried it was going to snow. If it snowed, they would leave footprints, not to mention hoofprints—a worrying thought. The alarm clock had awoken her from a heavy sleep. She had thought it must have roused the whole house, but no—not a sound anywhere. She had slipped out easily. A burglar could have a field day in their house, the way they all slept like the dead. Ros felt

K. M. PEYTON

slightly indignant—cheated almost—that her dangerous mission proved so easy.

Waiting wasn't good for the spirit. Ros felt herself becoming increasingly annoyed and nervous. The burning zeal of adventure was slithering away into cold, damp annoyance.

There seemed to be no cars on the road. Far

away a dog barked. Ros could hear her own breath on the cold air.

Suddenly there was an almighty clang of metal on concrete, very close. Ros nearly leapt out of her skin. It was the Crosses' garbage can, overturned on the concrete path and the round lid rolling backward and forward with a great racket. She heard Leo's squeak of alarm, and at the same time the upstairs window opened and Mr. Cross's uncertain voice shouted, "Who's there?"

Ros froze, her heart hammering.

How lucky it was so dark! Leo had flattened himself against the wall of the house, and had the sense to keep as still as a shadow. He was such an idiot Ros had half expected him to answer his father's question.

"It's a cat or something—a fox, perhaps," Mr. Cross called back to his wife. "Only the garbage can."

The window closed.

After a tense minute, Leo came down his garden path and slipped out of the gate. He was white and quivering, near to tears.

Ros, ready to castigate, decided encouragement would suit the situation better. "It's okay!

Don't worry. You were really clever to keep so still! Come on, there's nothing to be scared of."

She set off at a great pace, so he had no choice but to follow her. They had a bucket of food, and Ros had borrowed a head collar and lead rein from a girl in the grade above hers at school who had a pony. It would be a good clue for any police that might come snooping later, but Ros hadn't enough money to buy one—later would have to look after itself.

Leo stopped whimpering and cheered up when he discovered how empty the world was. The way was so familiar, the darkness did not hinder them. Only one car came down the road, and its headlights swung past as they waited in the shadow of the hedge.

"All clear!" Ros called out.

They ran across the road and up over the railroad bridge. Ros was bursting with excitement. She felt no fear, only an enormous relief that the moment had come at last, to rescue Badger from his misery.

It was almost as if the pony was expecting them. He came toward them on his chain and Ros heard his soft rippling nicker of greeting. Leo held the bucket up to him but Ros said sharply, "No, you've got to save it for the bridge, in case he won't go over." But Badger, having smelled the food, almost pulled the tether pin out of the ground to get to it. Leo backed off nervously. Badger started to paw the ground, ripping up clods of mud.

"Oh, shut up, Badger! We're going to give it to you!"

Ros fastened the head collar behind his ears, and tried to unbuckle the leather neck strap. But Badger was pulling on it so hard, she couldn't release the buckle.

"Here, Leo, you'll have to let him have a noseful."

With the pony's head in the bucket, she was able to get the strain off the collar, and the rusted buckle came undone after some bruising effort. The chain dropped on the ground with a satisfying clank. Ros picked up the lead rein firmly.

"Go on, Leo, get a move on. Walk in front."

The food was nearly all gone and they hadn't started off yet. Leo backed off and Badger plunged after him. Ros held the rope firmly, trying not to get her feet trodden on. Even thin and poor as the pony was, he still felt terribly strong on the end of the rope and Ros began to feel worried. She couldn't get him to take his nose out of the bucket, and by the time they got to the bottom of the footbridge steps the carrots were all eaten.

"Go on ahead," Ros said to Leo. With luck the pony would go on following the bucket.

She started to lead him purposefully, and to her immense relief he started quite willingly up the wide steps. But when he got to the top he stopped, and would not go on. Leo held out the bucket in vain. Ros tugged at the head collar but Badger stood like a rock.

"Please, Badger! We want to help you!"

Couldn't he understand? The more Ros tugged, the more firmly he stood. He stuck his front feet out and stubbornly resisted.

"Badger!" Ros's voice rose in a wail of despair.

Leo pushed behind and tried hitting him with the bucket, but Badger would not move.

"Oh, what shall we do?"

They had stopped whispering and being secret, for they had the night to themselves. But below them, beyond the railroad, two cars went by, and in the distance they could hear a faint clanking, as if from the switchyard.

"It's a train," Leo said.

"They don't come during the night!"

"The gravel train does," Leo said solemnly. "Every night at two o'clock."

"I've never heard it!"

"You're always asleep then. I have."

"Why didn't you warn me?"

"I thought you knew."

The noise of the approaching train was now quite distinct. Ros could feel the vibration of it in the soles of her rubber boots. Badger stopped being mulish and pricked his ears, lifting his head. Ros clung to the rope grimly.

"What shall we do?"

She could hear it now quite plainly, a heavy diesel train, traveling fast. Badger swung his head, obviously nervous. He backed a few steps and his back feet slipped off the top step.

"Oh, come on, Badger! Quickly, before it comes!"

But there was nothing she could do. The train came with a roar and the whole bridge shook. Badger plunged and snatched at the lead rope. Ros hung on grimly but was thrown on her face as Badger took off at a wild gallop. She let go with a shriek. Badger tore across the top of the bridge as the train thundered underneath, and Ros saw his muddy white tail disappear in a swirl as he galloped headlong down the steps on the other side.

"Badger, stop! Stop!"

Ros got up and ran. Leo sprinted after her, leaving the bucket bouncing behind. They got to the far side of the bridge in time to see Badger, having lost his footing, scrambling to his feet at the bottom of the steps.

"Badger, please! Badger, stop! Oh, do stop!"

But Ros could tell the pony was thoroughly alarmed, as much at being loose as by the train, and, with an excited tossing of his muddy mane, he started to trot along ahead of them. He trotted out onto the main road and turned up along the highway, in the opposite direction from what Ros intended, rope lead trailing.

"Oh, he'll be killed if a car comes!" Ros shrieked.

She ran as fast as she could, but Badger wasn't stopping. He didn't gallop, but just kept ahead, trotting fast. Ros was terrified. All thoughts of keeping hidden and secret had flown on the wind. Her expedition had taken off and was out of her control. Even as she ran, the lights of an approaching car began to beam over the slight rise ahead. Her worst fears were

realized. Badger was on the wrong side, and the car was coming fast toward him.

Unlike trains, cars were familiar to Badger, and he did not turn and run. He stopped, and stood foursquare on the tarmac. The headlights picked him up and he looked for a moment like the old Badger, head up and eyes shining. The car swerved and braked. On the wet road it went into a screaming skid, slewing sideways and missing Badger by inches. Ros got a brief blurred glance of a man's white face, quite close, then the car was past, and did not stop. It straightened up and accelerated away. Badger meanwhile turned and leapt across the median and careered away into some bushes on the far side of the road.

"Come on!"

Ros ran too. She jumped the median and Leo followed. Ros was aching with cramp and fear and having no breath. This was nothing like she had planned. Secrecy was no longer the problem. The problem was getting Badger back.

"At least the train made him go!" Leo panted behind her.

But go where?

There was now no sign of him. They were on the far side of the road and with Ros's pocket flashlight they could see Badger's hoofmarks in the wet grass. The verge had been planted with trees and bushes but they weren't yet very big.

"He can't have gone far. Listen!"

They stood very still, and soon heard a bush-crashing noise quite nearby. Ros made for it, and found Badger eating twigs greedily, not at all upset by his adventure. When she made a dive for his head rope he made no move to run away again, but continued eating.

"Oh, Badger! Thank goodness!"

Ros leaned against the pony's warm shoulder, trembling now with relief.

"Suppose that car had hit him!"

"Or the car had turned over," Leo said with relish. "You'd have thought the driver would have stopped, wouldn't you?"

"He must have seen us. Suppose he's gone to the police station to report it?"

"They won't be open," Leo said. "Not at two-fifteen."

"Do you think so?"

"Yes, I'm sure."

He was making it up, but pleased to be impressing Ros. He was amazed to find that he was enjoying himself no end. This was miles better than being asleep, and more exciting than frogs. Leo had never done anything exciting in his whole life, only piano lessons and home-work and Sundays spent cleaning the car for his pocket money. His father's idea of a day out was going to watch a bowling match.

Ros, on the other hand, was not enjoying her-self at all, and was longing for the adventure to be over.

"However do we get to Sid the Pigman from here?"

She had intended to take the lane past their own cottages, the way she knew. But now they were about a mile along the main road in the wrong direction.

Leo sensed that Ros was losing her general's grip. His mind felt sharp and strong.

"We are quite close, if you think of it. Our lane comes in this direction—we were going to come this way, only over there." He pointed across the fields. "A little bit farther along here, a lane crosses this road underneath, through a tunnel. If we can get down there, we can easily get to Sid's. He's just a little way down the lane. Don't you remember, when they built this road, the farmer made them give him a tunnel?"

Yes, Ros did remember. Her father said it was a triumph against the superpowers. The superpowers hadn't wanted to waste money on a tunnel. They had wanted to block the lane off.

"If we can climb down into the lane, we'll be almost there."

Ros was grateful for Leo taking over, but very nervous as to whether the lane was where he thought it was.

"If you like, I'll walk on and find it, and you can stay here and let Badger go on eating. You're nice and hidden in the bushes."

"Don't you mind?"

"No."

"That's a good idea. Don't get seen, for goodness' sake!" Ros thought that drivers might stop if they saw a boy as small as Leo trotting alone alongside the highway at around two-thirty in the morning. The two of them weren't to know, either, if the man who nearly hit Badger might be reporting a loose pony on the road. On the telephone perhaps. Ros didn't think the police slept all night, in spite of what Leo said. That's when crimes were happening, surely. What they were doing was a crime, after all, and they certainly wouldn't have attempted it in broad daylight.

She watched Leo hurry off to find the tunnel. At least they were on the right side of the road, and with luck would only have to scramble down an embankment.

She felt shaky and a bit tearful, and didn't dare think about what she was doing. She was a thief! She was a criminal! That's how other people would see it. But Badger was freed from his horrible chain and eating happily, tearing at the grass underfoot. You could see he was starving by the eagerness with which he ate. Already he seemed to her to have perked up, unlike herself. She was now the one who felt she had her back to the wind and her tail between her legs.

Thank goodness she had Leo to help her. Nothing had gone according to plan. She thought back over their adventures, and realized that the bucket was missing. They must have dropped it on the bridge! They had left a glaring clue, one even the thickest detective could not fail to see!

By the time Leo came back, she felt close to tears.

"It's all right," he said. "It's just up the road. We have to climb down the bank when we get there."

He sounded cheerful, but not entirely convincing.

"It's worth a try," he said.

"What do you mean?"

"It might be a little difficult."

Ros tried not to panic. She didn't ask him why it might be a little difficult—she didn't really want to know. She pulled Badger's head out of the grass and led him back to the verge where it was clear of bushes.

There had been no cars for some time and she prayed it would stay the same until they were safely out of sight again. A police car might come along . . .

But Badger was being very good and came along willingly. Ros told Leo about the bucket.

"I'll go back and get it afterward," he said.

He wanted the night to go on forever. It was magic. When they saw the first gleam of approaching headlights, he helped Ros get Badger hidden in the bushes again. Luckily only one car came, and then after a few minutes' walking they came to the tunnel. Ros saw at once the reason for Leo's doubt.

The lane, deep in its cutting below them, had banks heavily covered in brambles, hawthorn, oak saplings, and nettles. To get down the bank, they first had to get through a fence. The stout wooden fence that followed the road veered around and went away down the lane on the top of the bank, but two strands of barbed wire on a few posts were stretched across to the parapet of the bridge, cutting off their way.

"However do we get through there?" Ros wailed.

The verge was narrow at this point and they were standing in full view of any headlights that might come along. Ros felt her remaining courage fast draining away.

"It's rusty old stuff," Leo said. "I'll try and break it."

Badger started tearing at the grass again. Apart from the noise of his eating, the night was silent now and strangely hostile. The clouds covered the moon, but its brightness still shone eerily on the concrete ribbon of the road. The lane below was like a black pit. Ros could feel her heart thudding with fear, and she knew she was now depending entirely on Leo. He had managed to pull one of the posts out of the ground. If he stood on it, the barbed-wire strands were stretched almost to the ground.

"Will he step over?"

Ros hauled Badger's head off the grass.

"Come on, Badger! You've got to come!"

She stepped over the wires and pulled him after her. He hesitated, stopped.

"Badger!"

The way ahead was not inviting, not compared with the juicy roadside grass. Leo bent down and pulled up handfuls of grass, passed them to Ros.

"Hold these in front of him!"

Badger stretched out his neck, took one step.

"Please, Badger!"

Ros stepped back and Badger followed. Leo could not move for standing on the wire. Badger stepped over and stood with only one hind leg on the wrong side.

"Come on!"

A gleam in the distance warned of the approach of another car. It was on their side of the road.

Leo bent down and heaved at the laggard fetlock. Ros jerked on the lead rope.

Badger walked on, but his hind leg was caught up. Leo gave him a great slap on the backside and he plunged mightily, bringing the whole fence with him. Ros went over backward into the stinging nettles and Badger jumped over her with the whole fence behind him, posts and all.

Ros screamed.

The car swept past, not noticing the drama at all.

The barbed wire broke and Badger kicked himself free, and went plunging on down through the undergrowth with the same abandon he had shown earlier. Ros had let him go again, and now found herself weeping with fright and the nettles.

"It's all right!" Leo was shouting. "We're through!"

"He's gone!"

"Not far, I bet. And it doesn't matter down here! We'll find him. Come on, Ros—we've done all the hard parts!"

It was all right for Leo—he hadn't fallen in the nettles. Ros staggered to her feet and beat her way down the bank, choking with pain and anxiety. If only the night was over!

"Where is he?"

The lane was dark and muddy, but at last they were hidden and safe. Ros straightened up, rubbing her tingling face, and felt herself coming together again, after the panics. Leo was right. They had done the bad parts.

With her flashlight, they found Badger's hoofprints in the mud, going down the lane.

"He's gone the right way this time."

"He'll stop at the first grass he comes to."

Leo's words proved right. As the lane opened out away from the tunnel cutting, the wooded banks gave way to grassy verge and trimmed hedges, and there was Badger grazing again, lead rope trailing. He let Ros catch him, still eating.

"Thank goodness for that!" Ros examined his legs with her flashlight, and found a few bleeding gouges on one back leg, but not deep enough to worry about. His freedom was worth a scratch or two. She was sure he would think so.

They only had a few hundred yards to go down the lane. The woods that screened Sid's place from the road made a dark blot to the right. To the left, across the open fields, Ros knew their own row of cottages lay—not more than ten minutes' walk away.

Now she was ashamed of being frightened. It was Leo who had risen to the occasion. The generalship had changed hands. She felt humbled, and warm with gratitude toward Leo. But she didn't say anything.

"I hope his dogs don't bark," Leo whispered.

But greyhounds aren't guard dogs. They slept in an elegant heap on Sid's bed, keeping him warm. Leo and Ros crept past, and Badger followed them, quiet now, and trusting. The cow and the donkey were in the barn, both lying down, and the gate at the bottom of the field swung easily as Leo pulled back the catch.

Ros led Badger through and took off his head collar. She retreated, and Leo shut the gate silently behind her.

Badger started to graze, not stopping to explore his new surroundings. He did not bother to buck and kick and gallop about; he just wanted to eat. The cow and the donkey, undisturbed, did not even get up.

Ros stood watching him, with large tears rolling down her cheeks. She wept with gratitude to see her pony in his lovely new surroundings, with plenty to eat and a stream to drink from, and a cow and a donkey for companions. As if in celebration, the moon came out from behind the clouds and shone brightly on her wonderful achievement.

CHAPTER

6

Now that it was over, Ros felt very strange, weepy and yet, at the same time, elated, shivering with pride and excitement. They had done it!

She also felt very cold, tired and sore. Her face burned with nettle stings. She wanted desperately to be back in her warm bed.

"But they'll see the fence! And we left the bucket—"

"I'll see to all that," Leo said grandly.

"What do you mean?"

"I'll go and do it now. I'll stamp out the hoofprints, put the fence back, get the bucket—so nobody will know!"

"What, by yourself?"

"Yes."

"Aren't you afraid?"

"No."

Ros couldn't believe it. She, General Palfrey, had been afraid. Very much so, in fact. But little squirty Leo, who never said boo to a goose, was acting six feet tall. His face in the moonlight seemed to glow.

"I'll come back with you first, if you like," he said.

Ros was grateful. She seemed to have run out of both nerve and energy. She had the shivers. They started for home, which was only ten minutes' walk away, but seemed anything but familiar. The moon had now decided to reveal itself, and rode serenely above the winter fields. It was bitterly cold, which Ros hadn't noticed before. When they got to the turning into the lane where they lived, Leo stopped.

"I'll go back now. Can I have the flashlight?"

Ros handed it over. "How long will you be? You mustn't be found out!"

Leo shone the flashlight on his watch. "It's only three o'clock. It won't take long."

"And you can get in all right?"

"Yes. I've got the key."

"Be careful, then." But even as she said it, she knew she spoke only out of habit. Leo laughed.

Ros crept home. She slipped in like a shadow,

feeling the warmth and security of her house folding her in, seeing Erm's welcoming tail, the kitchen table set for breakfast, hearing the comfortable ticking of the hall clock. She was so relieved, she felt the feeble tears sliding down her cheeks again. She crawled up the stairs on all fours and tiptoed into her bedroom. The moon shone in, a stranger now, visiting from another world. She stood looking out for a moment, trying to take in the amazing adventure of her night. She had stolen Badger—it had worked, her plan, and he was rescued from the terrible Dad Smith and his miserable life. Beneath her incredible weariness, this knowledge was warm and secure. She was too tired now to wonder what might happen next. She rolled into bed and fell fast asleep.

And while Ros slept, Leo cavorted through the night. He stamped down the hoofprints in the lane, he pushed the fence posts back in the ground and hooked the broken wire together; he brushed away all the hoofprints along the verge, hid from several passing cars, and made his way back to the railroad bridge. It took him ages to find the bucket, as it had rolled down the steps and halfway down the railroad bank, but after he had retrieved it he went back to Badger's chain and obliterated all the marks that led to the railroad bridge.

Then he stood on the railroad bridge and looked up at the moon, and all around at the brightly lit, silent, sleeping world, and he felt a great burst of joy surging out of his chest and

into his throat so that he had to open his mouth
to let it out. He stood on the bridge and yelled.
His voice was like a trumpet: a fanfare to de-
light.

"Hooray! Hooray! Hooray!" he shouted.

And nothing moved. The road, the railroad
were still, like a stage set, and—stagiest of all—
the great white moon shining overhead. Leo
had never been out alone at night before. He felt
he had never done anything before, not anything at all. He had been asleep all his life, compared with how he felt now. He never wanted to
go to bed again. He didn't want to go home. He
wanted to stand on the bridge and shout. So he
did, until a distant beam showed a car coming.
It had a blue light on top, revolving. It was a
police car. Leo ducked down and stayed silent
on the bridge until it had passed. Perhaps it was
looking for Badger? But it would never find him.
Only someone in rubber boots could find Badger, and there were no signs anymore of the
way he had gone.

"Hooray!" shouted Leo.

He ran across the bridge with the bucket and
jumped down the steps to the bottom. It seemed
a great pity, but there didn't seem to be anything else to do anymore. To spin it out, Leo

walked back up the road, to go back past Badger, the way they had taken earlier. He sang as he walked, "Green Grow the Rushes, O," but couldn't remember after "Seven for the seven stars in the sky," so started on a song his father sang while he was in the bath: "My name is MacNamara, I'm the leader of the band." But the cars were getting more frequent now and he had to hide six times before he got to the lane. He slid down the far side, to make a change, and then walked silently in case the greyhounds heard him.

Badger was still grazing ravenously, and the cow and the donkey were out now and grazing near him. They were all quite friendly by the look of it. Badger did not even lift his head as Leo hung over the gate.

Leo left the bucket inside the gate for Sid and went on home. At last he was feeling tired. But magnificently tired, as he had never felt before, tired like a giant, with a great giant weariness, and a great giant content. The lane was dark and silent. Nothing stirred. Leo went in like a burglar, quiet as a cat.

Perhaps that's what I'll be—a burglar, he thought.

Then he thought, I am. And slept.

Next day it snowed, deep and thick. It was almost Christmas. Ros knew they couldn't have done it now, not in the snow, and was deeply, deeply happy. Underneath, that is. On top, she was jumpy with nerves, waiting for a policeman to knock on the door, or Dad Smith to telephone. Her mother thought she was coming down with something. She was white-faced and twitchy, and kept getting the shivers. Some general! She didn't dare go over the railroad bridge, in case she met Dad Smith discovering his pony had been stolen. She kept wondering what he was doing about it. Even if he had discovered it yet. He didn't come every day, not now that he knew Albert filled the water bucket.

The police didn't come, and nobody rang up.

Ros lay low for the whole of the next day, yawning a lot, but the day after, when nothing had happened, she decided to venture out. She couldn't help wanting to see Badger again, to see that he was still there. For all she knew, Dad Smith had found him and taken him away.

Leo said, "Return to the scene of the crime—that's what murderers do."

"No one'll see us. Nobody goes up there."

"We'll leave tracks."

They went, all the same. It was still snowing. "Our tracks'll get covered up."

But they made deep, bluish scars in the untouched snow. The tractor tracks had browned the lane where it left their houses, but after they had passed the riding school and the turning to the farm, the small lane up to the tunnel was unmarked, a pure white river running between the jagged darkness of the bare hedges. At the top they could see the dark hole of the tunnel, and hear the distant hum of the traffic behind the trees.

"When Sid goes out, he goes under the tunnel. He doesn't come this way," Leo said.

"Nobody comes this way," Ros said.

"If you were a detective in Siberia, or Alaska, it would all be quite easy," Leo said, looking back with satisfaction at their trail. He was full of confidence. He stamped his feet and made flurries in the snow. He turned around and walked backward.

"That's a way to trick them. They think you're going the other way. I should've worn my father's rubber boots. That would've fooled them still more."

"They'd have fallen off."

Leo started making very long strides. "I'm a little man with very long legs, they'll think."

"And a small brain," Ros said, getting rather annoyed at Leo's tricks.

The cold air stung her face, making her eyes water. The sky was brownish, and the falling flakes white and soft, wet on her cheeks. But there was no wind, and the hedges stood stark, holding the snow in their arms. Where there was a gap in the hedge, the snow had drifted deep. Ros shivered, frightened for Badger. She was desperate to see if he was all right.

But when they came to the stream at the bottom of Sid's field, they saw Badger standing at the top with the cow and the donkey. They were all eating hay, which had been set out separately in three piles.

"*Three* piles!" Ros whispered.

Sid had taken Badger. He was feeding him. He hadn't taken him to the police station.

Relief filled her, swamping her shivers and jitters. She leaned on the gate, watching how eagerly Badger was eating the good hay. It wasn't the moldy stuff Dad Smith had supplied. He was gobbling it up. Ros wanted to go up the field to talk to him, but didn't dare.

"I bet he'll come if you call him," Leo said.

"No, we shouldn't let Sid see us."

She thought she could see Sid's face in the trailer window, and turned to go home, nervous again. Their tracks in the snow seemed to shout to the sky—"Look what we've done!"

Their plan had worked better than she had ever dreamed. Yet the success did not seem to make her happy, not even after seeing Badger. She still felt nervous and guilty. She kept wanting to go and visit Badger, to see he was still there, but every time she felt worse, instead of better. Her parents thought she was ill. She couldn't eat. She kept thinking of Dad Smith arriving at the door, full of his terrible rage. She discovered that she was no general. It was Leo who had turned into a general, suddenly a new boy, full of confidence.

Ros's parents thought she was feverish.

"I shall have to take you to the doctor," her mother said. "I can't think what's wrong with you. It's three days now—picking at your food! And you look like a ghost."

Ros said nothing. Her father was giving her thoughtful looks, saying nothing too.

In the evening the phone rang. Her mother answered it, and shouted to her father, who was watching television, "It's for you. A Mr. Smith."

Ros let out a choking cry and rushed out of the room. She fled up to the bathroom and locked herself in. All she could think of was the red, aggressive face looming over her at the horse show, the beefy arm raised, the awful threats. Yet, even being so afraid, the thought of Badger in Sid's lovely field gave her a deep feeling of defiance. It's Badger who matters, she thought. Even being so afraid, she wouldn't have changed anything. She sat on the edge of the bath, trying to be brave, and not being very successful.

The phone call seemed to take a long time. She sat there realizing that it was all up, and that she had to face the consequences, and that she now had an even harder job on her hands to save Badger. The thought of Dad Smith taking him back was unbearable. Instead of crying and shivering, she did her best to stiffen herself into a figure of resolution and courage. It was extremely difficult. She went on sitting on the edge of the bath. Outside it was dark and snowing again.

After a long time her father came upstairs and called her name. She didn't answer. He tried the bathroom door.

"Ros?"

"Dad." Softly.

"What's wrong?"

Surely he knew?

"Let me in."

She got up and unlocked the door. Her father looked down at her curiously. He looked so sympathetic and reliable that her newfound courage gave way and she burst into tears. He put his arms around her and she buried her face in the front of his pullover. She wept.

"What's it all about?"

"What did—what did he say? Mr. . . . Mr. Smith—"

"Mr. Smith? He said he was sorry he hadn't been in to service the boiler but his wife's had to go to the hospital with blood pressure and they've decided to keep her in until the baby's born, and that means there's no one at home to look after their old gran and one way or another it's a little difficult to get away just now, but with luck he'll get around in another week or two. Why do you want to know?"

Ros took her face out of her father's pullover and looked up at him, amazed.

"He—it was—wasn't—it wasn't *that* Mr. Smith?"

"What Mr. Smith?"

"The one who owns Badger?"

"No. Why should it be?"

"Oh—oh! Oh, Dad!"

Ros flung her arms round him, half crying, half laughing. He held her, and laughed too.

"What's all this about? What's gotten into you, Rosalind Palfrey?"

So she told him. She told him everything that had happened.

CHAPTER

7

The next day was Christmas Eve. Harry Palfrey decided to take the day off.

"We'll go for a walk, you and me," he said to Ros.

"Where to?"

Ros was still dithery, although unloading all her cares onto her father had made her feel very much better, and hungry again. She had bacon and eggs for breakfast. Surprisingly, neither of her parents had said very much about what she had done. Not to her, at least. When she was in bed, she had heard them talking in the room below, right up until she fell asleep.

"We'll go up and have a chat with Sid, I thought."

He fetched his rubber boots out of the garage.

"Can Leo come?"

"Of course."

But Leo was having a piano lesson.

His backward footsteps still showed in the snow. As he had walked backward both ways, his footsteps looked just the same as Ros's, who had walked forward.

"Ages since I've been up here," Harry said cheerfully, as they plowed up the lane. Big dollops of thawing snow fell on them from the branches above. The air was softer, and crows wheeled, black as coal, against the damp gray sky. This time they did not stop at the bottom of the field, but went on up the lane toward the tunnel, to where the trailer stood with its back to the trees and the road. Badger was in the barn still eating. They went in the gate and up the ash path to the trailer door. Sid was just coming out, cap pulled well down, dirty muffler tied around his neck. He was a small, quiet man with gaps in his teeth, brown like a gypsy, neither young nor old. He had a thin cigarette hanging from his lower lip.

"Good morning," Harry said.

Sid did not answer, just looked.

"It's about the piebald pony."

"Aye?"

"My daughter here put it in your field."

"Did she now?"

Sid stood with his hands in his pockets, and stared at Ros. He had dark brown eyes, very shiny and quick, like a small animal used to living by its wits.

"She took it from its tether by Safeway's parking lot and put it here because she thought it was being ill-treated. Not a very smart thing to do."

Sid went on looking at Ros, till she felt embarrassed. Then he winked at her.

To Harry he said, shifting his cigarette to one side, "I wouldn't say that."

"I want to straighten it out. She's stolen it, and put the onus on you. You could be in trouble for receiving stolen goods. We wouldn't want that to happen."

Sid chewed on the end of his cigarette once more.

He grinned. "Wouldn't be the first time."

"You reckon it's all right for the pony to stay here for the time being, then, while I see the police?"

He hadn't mentioned the police to Ros, up till now. At the dread word, all Ros's shivers came back.

"Dad!"

"Why bring the police into it?" Sid said.

Ros's feelings exactly.

"Get it straightened out," Harry said.

"We've straightened it out," Sid said. "That man . . . kept it on that tether—he don't deserve no pony."

"Oh, he doesn't! Dad, he doesn't!" Ros could see that Sid was exactly the right sort of man.

"I agree. All the same, it needs to be straightened out." Harry's voice was very firm.

Sid shrugged. "Suit yourself. Nobody's bin looking, mind you. Ask 'em first, if it's bin reported missing. It wasn't treated like a pony anyone cared about. Anyone wanted, like."

"That's perfectly true."

Ros could see that Sid was a man after her own heart.

"Oh, Dad, don't tell them what I did!"

"Stupid, that'd be," Sid said.

Harry stood there, considering.

"There's more wrong on their side than there is on the littl'un's here. I saw that pony. Wicked neglect, that was."

"Well—" Harry stood staring across the fields, at a loss now. "You're quite right. But—all the same—I'm not having my child breaking the law."

"She done right, pal. But suit yourself."

Sid shrugged again.

"I got work to do," he said, and left them, walking away under the tunnel.

Harry and Ros stood in the cold air, looking after him. Ros was tingling with half fear, half excitement.

"Oh, Dad!"

Ros could not express her feelings; she had the shivers. Harry put his arm around her shoulders and gave her a little hug.

"Can I give Badger his carrots?" She broke away and ran across the grass toward the wire fence that kept the animals off the trailer. She called Badger and he came out of the barn, head up, ears pricked, recognizing her voice. He came over to the fence and gave her his little nickering noise of welcome, and she flung her arms around his neck.

"Oh, you like it here, Badger, don't you? I'll never let them take you away, I promise!"

Her father watched her, his eyes full of anxiety. Even he could see that Badger was already showing his old spark, freed of his tether and fed for three days on good food. He was still a ragbag of staring ribs and dull, matted coat, but his expression was bright, his ears all optimism. The awful dejection, tail to wind and snow, was no longer apparent.

Harry could not bear the thought of breaking Ros's heart.

He stood looking at his feet, at the patterns his rubber boot soles made in the snow. In the trailer, four sleek greyhounds watched him out of the window. The crows wheeled against the sky.

"What are you going to do, Dad?" Ros asked anxiously as they walked home.

"I'm thinking about it."

They passed the farm turning and the riding school, and followed the slushy tractor tracks. Harry walked in silence.

When they got home, he turned to Ros and said, "We've got to go to the police, Ros. I'm sorry. As it stands, you're a thief. I can't just accept that my daughter is a thief. If everyone took what they wanted, how could we get on in this life? It's a very basic law, not to take other people's property. I believe in it, and you must too."

"But—"

"I know you did it for Badger. All right. What Sid says is true—that you did a good thing rather than a bad thing. But you're still a thief.

It's a real mess, like a whole lot of things that happen. There's no exact answer. So, as Sid seems to have a pretty sensible outlook on life, we'll do what he suggests, go to the police and inquire if Badger's disappearance has been reported. And go from there."

"Do you really think Mr. Smith might not have reported it?"

"I don't know. Looking after the pony was obviously a great drag, as far as he was concerned. He might be glad to be rid of him. And there's nothing in the local paper about a pony being stolen. So it could be . . ."

Harry got the car out when they got home, and told Ros to hop in. They drove to the police station. Ros had gotten the big shivers by now, and sat huddled down under her seatbelt, listening to her heart thumping with apprehension.

"What are you going to say?"

"Ask if a piebald pony has been reported missing."

"Not say where it is!"

"No, just say we saw the tether lying, and wondered if it had gotten away. We're worried about its safety."

"What if they say yes, and what do you know about it?"

"I'll prevaricate."

"What does that mean?"

"Make it up as I go along."

He gave her a quick hug and got out of the car. She watched him disappear into the police station.

Oh, Badger! Ros sat trembling. It was the worst feeling she had ever had in her life, even worse than when she had attacked Dad Smith at the horse show.

It felt like hours.

Her father came out and straight across to the car.

"What do you think? They've never heard of him. No word of a piebald pony stolen, nothing at all."

"You mean—"

"It means he never reported it. Which seems to me, he doesn't care. He's glad to be rid of him."

"Oh, Dad!"

Ros didn't know whether to laugh or cry. Badger could stay in his lovely field with kind, sensible Sid and the cow and the donkey and the barnful of good hay! He would grow round and fat and shining again, and have strength to gallop and kick up his heels. He would never whinny in the night again, stranded on his tether without food and shelter.

"Sid can keep him! He *wants* him—you can tell. He likes him, doesn't he?"

"I certainly got that impression."

"Can we go and tell him?"

"We'll go back this afternoon."

Ros sat in the car feeling as if all her senses were zinging. Her head reeled. Her father was laughing—he was as relieved as she was. When they got home they told the story to Dora Palfrey, and then Leo came around, hot-cheeked and said, "Guess what?"

"What?"

"I came home from Safeway's this morning and I met Albert—you know, with the dog—and he said he saw Mr. Smith come with some rotten old hay for Badger, and when he saw he'd gone he just collected up the chain and the tether pin and said to Albert, 'Good riddance!' and drove away!"

"Well, that just about buttons it up," Harry said.

Ros told Leo about visiting Sid and the police station.

"Sid wants him, and now he can have him. Can't he, Dad? It's all right?"

"It sounds all right to me."

"It's very all right," Leo said.

"And we can visit him every day."

After lunch they all went back to tell Sid what had happened. The snow was falling—it was going to be a white Christmas. But a happy white Christmas. Ros was bursting with happiness. She could never have enjoyed the snow if Badger had still been standing there abandoned beside the railroad line. He came for her carrots, and pushed his soft lips at her pockets and Sid stood watching them, chewing his cigarette.

"Ponies need work," he said. "I might get him a cart, and do some scrap collecting. I did that once. There's money in it, close to a town like this. He's just right for that. He'd like that. Now he's mine, like."

"Well, yes, we'd like you to keep him, now that it seems all straight with the police."

"You might meet Mr. Smith, when he's in the cart," Ros said dubiously.

Sid grinned. "I know how to handle the likes of Mr. Smith!"

"I can come and see him?"

"Every day, pal."

The carrots were all gone and it was beginning to get dark. The headlights of the cars on

the main road made distant weaving patterns through the leafless trees and the snow was growing crunchy underfoot. Ros went home with her father, thinking about Badger. She had had a dream of riding him one day . . .

"I wish—"

"I know, love."

They turned out of Sid's lane toward home.

"He's happy. That's what matters. And pulling a cart is a good job for a pony—steady, slow work . . . horses thrive on that. You know the old canal horses, that pulled the barges, used to live till forty, it suited them so."

What odd things her father did know.

"Do you think it will suit Badger?"

"Better than show jumping."

Ros remembered the day at the show, and shivered.

Badger had gotten his Christmas and was going to stay lucky, she knew that now. And she had gotten very nearly everything she had ever wanted. No one ever got *everything* after all—how dull that would be. She gave a little skip in the snow, and her father laughed.

"Merry Christmas!"

Merry Christmas after all.

About the Author

A winner of the Carnegie Medal, K. M. Peyton is the author of the Flambards trilogy, recently dramatized and shown on PBS. Delacorte Press has published her young adult novel *Darkling*. K. M. Peyton lives in Essex, England, where she rides regularly. She has a half share in a race horse currently in training.

About the Illustrator

Mary Lonsdale is a young illustrator who graduated with a degree in Graphic Design and Illustration from Bristol Polytechnic in Avon, England, in 1989. An animal lover, she has two dogs. She lives in the West Midlands and is at work on several more projects.